Gertie's Birthday Hiccups

by Liza Charlesworth

ISBN: 978-1-338-89045-7

Designer: Cynthia Ng; Illustrated by John Lund

1 2 3 4 5 6 7 8 9 10   68   31 30 29 28 27 26 25 24 23 22

Printed in Jiaxing, China. First printing, January 2023.

In a cozy home, there lived
a sweet green monster named Gertie.
Today she was 10 years old!
Gertie was VERY excited
except for one thing....

She had a bad case of the birthday hiccups.
How could she get rid of them?
Then, Gertie had a great idea.
"I will ask my brother," she said.

3

Gertie found her brother in his bedroom.
"Do you know how to cure a bad case
of the birthday hiccups?" she asked.
"Yup!" responded her brother.
"Hold your nose and hop on my bed."

So Gertie gave it a try.
She held her nose and
hopped on his bed.
Did the cure work? NOPE.
"Sorry!" said her brother. "Go ask Mom."

Gertie found her mom in the living room.
"Do you know how to cure a bad case
of the birthday hiccups?" she asked.
"Sure do!" responded her mom.
"Do jumping jacks and sing the Alphabet Song."

So Gertie gave it a try.
She did jumping jacks and
sang the Alphabet Song.
Did the cure work? NOPE.
"Oh dear!" said her mom. "Go ask Dad."

Gertie found her dad in the kitchen.
"Do you know how to cure a bad case
of the birthday hiccups?" she asked.
"That's easy!" responded her dad.
"Waddle around and quack like a duck."

So Gertie gave it a try.
She waddled around and
quacked like a duck.
Did the cure work? NOPE.
"Yikes!" said her dad. "Go ask Grandma."

Gertie found her grandma in the backyard.
"Do you know how to cure a bad case
of the birthday hiccups?" she asked.
"Indeed!" said her grandma. "Sit down,
close your eyes tight, and count to 1,000."

Grandma's cure was the oddest one of all.
But she had nothing to lose,
so Gertie decided to give it a try.
She closed her eyes and
counted all the way to 1,000.

"I don't think your cure worked!" said Gertie.
"That's OK," responded her grandma.
"You can open your eyes now."
When Gertie did, she heard a VERY loud...

"SURPRISE!!!!!"
She saw her grandma, dad, mom, and brother.
She saw a card and gifts and balloons.
She saw a pretty cake with ten candles.

WOW! Gertie was so shocked,
she fell right off her chair.
What did Gertie NOT do? HICCUP!
At last, her birthday hiccups were cured.

"I was so surprised when you yelled 'SURPRISE!'
that my hiccups went away!" exclaimed Gertie.
"I thought that might work," said her grandma.
"Now, it's time for you to celebrate."

So Gertie made a wish and blew
out every one of her candles.
"Hip, Hip, Hooray!" shouted her family.
Then, Gertie, the sweet green monster,
had a VERY happy hiccup-less birthday.